SADIE the GOAT
by Max Sparber

ISBN: 9781798277836

TABLE OF CONTENTS

THE BALLAD OF SADIE THE GOAT

There's a figure doubled over
in the alley by the square
some wonder if she's breathing,
but they leave her lying there
none goes to see about her
none calls to her, none dare
though she's old and arthritic
and her clothes she ragged wear

there's a boy he's crossing to her
and he kneels and prods her now
the boy's mother she calls to him
don't you touch her don't nohow
but the boy he does not listen
Puts his hand upon her brow
O and both are quiet briefly
in the shadows in the slough

look she's dead he cries now
look her lips are tight and blue
and the boy he tugs upon her
saying let's take a look at you
and his mother she cries leave her
leave her be boy come here do
but the boy he stand up curious
and takes in a better view

she's just another body
in a fourth ward full of dead
and dead bodies have full pockets
that should be emptied out instead
a nickel will buy you roast beef
and a penny will buy you bread
a corpse with a full pocket
is a boy who sleeps unfed

and this corpse has got a locket
hanging from a golden chain
it's a battered wooden box
that has clattered in the drain
but it must be a thing of value
to be hung from such a chain
and so the boy kicks at the box
and then he kicks and kicks again

its shatters and it opens
and the boy he stoops to see
the contents of the box now
and he grasps out greedily
and his mother she calls to him
do not touch it leave it be
but the boy he does not listen
and his hands they grasp gladly

it's an ear he cries out mother
it's an ear an ear an ear
and he drops it and runs to her
and she swats him on his rear
and says I told you didn't I eh
I told you to come here
I should beat you but anyway
you nearly caught your death from fear

and the body lies untouched
in an alley on a furrow
and the mother pulls her son away
saying come now lad let's go now
who was she he asks weeping
oh she says, oh, oh, oh now
she was a pirate she was a pirate
and that's all you need to know now

IN THE AULD FOURTH WARD

My name's Sadie Farrell
And I'm just now sixteen
I was born in the Fourth Ward
To Molly O'Breen
I was born in a crimp house
Above Cherry Street
And me pa was a sailor
And we ain't never meet

It's the city Manhattan
It's the lower east side
A tenement on one end
A river beside
Here's Sweeny's Shambles
Where people pile like cords
You live and you die fast
In the auld fourth ward

What use is for children
But to sell or be sold
Most die of jail fever
Before one year old
Some make it like I did
By tooth and by nail
Some work as a roller
Some work as a tail

Every third word is Irish
Every accent a brogue
Each song is of Ireland
From each degenerate rogue
They sing and they weep some
The whiskey pours pours pours poured
None expected to be here
In the auld fourth ward

The rozzers don't come here
Unless armed and six strong
So it's all pandemonium
Rantam scantam lifelong
We does what we wants to
And we're done unto too
You're known by your woundings
And the scars they give you

There's lads in the streets now
Top hats and long tails
Lads under the docks
Telling stories of jail
They plot they will blag some
Like me each is scarred
I want to plot with them
In the auld fourth ward

FOUR STORIES ABOUT LETTERS

I

Most ain't got no learning
Most they cannot spell
Most ain't got no interest
And no ambition to as well
They does what they does
And they is what they was
And anything else
Anything else
Everything else
Can go to hell

II

A boy named Johnny Greely
Was a newsboy for the Sun
And he came back to the Fourth Ward
And learned reading O he done
And everybody in need
With a bill or a deed
They pay him
O they pay him
They pay Johnny
To read

III

The gangs all know of Johnny
There's the local police gazette
And when there's a new issue
Well it's Johnny O they get
And hour after hour
He reads of deeds both rank and sour
And buddy
Listen buddy
I know what that is
That is power

IV

I ain't got much money
I ain't barely earn a dime
But I will talk to Johnny
I will pay him for his time
For each penny that's conferred now
He'll teach letter and then word now

And in weeks
And in months
I'll be a thing that's
Unheard now

I'll be a girl what can read

BOOKS ABOUT PIRATES

Walk down Mott to Mulberry
There's a St. Pat church right there
And a school for Catholic girls
With lovely ribbons in their hair
And they read from books all year
Then they give the books away
And I'm Sadie and I can read

So I gets their charitay
I gets their charitay

And the priest he says now Sadie
What sort of books d'ya wanna read
And I say sure books on thieving
And he answers o indeed
We Irish know of larceny
As our Isle the British took
But I don't want to read of that

There's finer tales found in books
There's better things to read in books

And the priest he says now Sadie
Once pirates came to stay
And they ransacked all our churches
And they took our things away

He forgets that I'm a reader
All this I have done read
That the norsemen built up Dublin

And fathered Irish kings instead
They fathered Irish kings instead

Lochlann he was Viking
And Sitric and Magnus
Irish blood is made of pirate
There's pirate in all of us
When they fly the Jolly Roger
They fly Edward England's jack
And from Ireland he came

And his bone flag colored black
His bone flag colored black

And there was Edward Jordan
He was County Carlow's son
Until he raised up pirate colors
And held Halifax to the gun
I ain't never sailed the seas
And I ain't never shot a gun
But stealing from Canadians

That's one thing I have done
It's one thing I have done

And wasn't there two women
Who on pirate shores they docked
Yes, first came Grace O'Malley
The Sea Queen of Connaught
She sailed out of Clew Bay
Did from the Scottish steal
And she met with the Queen of England

And she refused to kneel
O Grace refused to kneel

And then there came Anne Bonney
Who at 13 stabbed a maid
I ain't never had a servant
But I have got a blade
Anne Bonney married a sailor
And burned her father's manse
And set sail then for Nassau

City of rum, pirates, and chance
City of rum, pirates, and chance

She sailed on the Revenge
And bedded with Calico Jack
And she strode it with her blouse off
And she never once looked back
They caught her in Jamaica
And put Jack to noose and flog
She said he was a man

They needn't hang him like a dog
They needn't hang him like a dog

And Anne Bonney she was sentenced
To be hanged up by her neck
For onerous acts of piracy
From the sloop Revenge's deck
And the day it came to hang her
And the gibbet was in the ground
And they went to find Anne Bonney

And Anne Bonney wasn't found
Anne Bonney was never found

This I read in books, sir
This is history
What came from Catholic schoolgirls
And was handed down to me
So I tell you this, o father
When you talk of Irish pain
That we Irish have been pirates
And we'll be pirates once again

We Irish have been pirates
I'll be a pirate if I can

A BROKEN ALPHABET OF GANGS

B is for the Batavia Street Gang
What robbed Siegel's jewelry store
To steal clothes for the Sullivan Ball
They took pride in all what they wore

And **B** is for the Baxter Street Dudes
The gang what run the Baxter Street Bar
But they also did plays and variety shows
And ran the Grand Duke Theat-ar

C is for Corcoran's Roosters
Who were also known as Rag Gang
They lived in shanties up on Dutch Hill
And told the cops to go hang

D is for the Daybreak Boys
You had to kill a man just to be one
Eventually the cops went after them armed
Saying kill one if'n you see one

And **D** is for the Dutch Mob of course
Each one was a pickpocket crook
They often liked to start fighting in streets
And rob those who stopped for a look

And **E** is for the Eastman Gang
Almost all Jews to the gent

Most worked as pimps on Rivington Street
Riding bicycles wherever they went

H is for the notorious Hook Gang
Who operated down by the wharf
They liked to hijack men rowing in boats
And make them row back and forth

M is for the Molasses Gang
Who wandered from ward to ward
Sometimes they'd start robbing a man
But then wander away from him, bored

N is for the 19th Gang
Who were vicious right down to the bone
Unless you were Catholic and could recite psalms
Then they'd bless you and leave you alone

S is for the slaughter house gang
Who organized bare-knuckle brawls
But don't let them follow you into a bar
Or they'll knife you through to the wall

T is for the Tub of Blood Bunch
Led by a man named Boru
He fell asleep once outside a bar
And the rats they ate him straight through

W is for the famous Whyos
An especially enterprising mob
$7 will pay for nose and jaw broke
But one hundred buys the big job

But **P** is for the Municipal Police
And **T** is for Tammany Hall
There's a lot of gangs in New Amsterdam
But they're the biggest gang of them all

RATS

If you want some sport
Some merry merry sport
There's the sportsman's Hall
Owned by our Kit Burns
Off on Water Streets
Two stuffed dogs are on its wall
Have a drink or two
Then lay down your coin
And tip back you hats
There's a pit in there
It's a bloody bloody pit
Where dogs get set on rats

Sing hey ho for our Kit Burns
And hey for the Sportmans Hall
A good dog will kill a hundred vermin
And the best will kill them all

He was in a gang
In a wicked wicked gang
In our own Roach Guard
Now he puts up fights
Bare knuckle brawls
Have men bruised, broke, and scarred
But the terriers O
The hungry hungry dogs
They are the kings of the show

So if you want some sport
Some merry merry sport
You know where you must go

Sing hey ho for our Kit Burns
And hey for the Sportmans Hall
A good dog will kill a hundred vermin
And the best will kill them all

THE GOAT

There's a man on Pearl Street
In top hat and tails
He's been drinking, he's drunk his share
Hear his cheers and wassails
I bet his pocket is full of coin
I bet there's quid in his coat
Someone needs to relieve him of that
Someone named Sadie the Goat

There's a sailor down Vandewater
Looking out for a skirt
A perfumed word and he's in the clouds
Just some eye bats and flirts
I bet you he's been paid this week
A note or at least a half note
It's bout time he was parted from that
And it went to Sadie the goat

All I needs is a chum with me
With a sap in his mitt
I butts my head into a chest
Me chum hits him a bit
We puts our hands into his vest
His pockets and all his clothes
Then we open up a sewer grate
And that's where he goes

There's a blade with a walking stick
And a raked bowler hat
He's flashing coin like he earned it all
Someone will relieve him of that
It just takes me hands on his buttoned vest
And me gloves on his throat
And he won't be conscious for too long
Not with Sadie the Goat

All I needs is a chum with me
With a sap in his mitt
I butts my head into a chest
Me chum hits him a bit
We puts our hands into his vest
His pockets and all his clothes
Then we open up a sewer grate
And that's where he goes

There's a copper on the beat
On Ferry and Gold
It's hard to work when he's around
It's hard for schemes to unfold
Get him before his whistle's out
Leave just his cap still afloat
Even policemen sometimes drown
Around Sadie the Goat

GALLUS MAG

We're all in the mood for a drink, yes
You want a drink, don't you
Well go ahead down water street
To the Hole in the Wall, won't you
The company there is the city's best
If you like your company low
If you want your rum spiked with mayhem
Or a splash oh of blood in pernod

It ain't been the same since Patsy the Barber
Took a straight razor to Slobbery Jim
We all agree that it ain't been the same
It's gotten much madder since he gave him a trim
The owner's a man he's one-armed Charley
And he has a taste for the breaking of bone
But if there's to be violence in Charley's saloon
Charley wants the mayhem to be all his own

Charley he hired him two vicious bruisers
Giants they are, both over six feet
Both are well-skilled in the art of shanghai-ing
Both claim half the murders along Dover Street
The first I grew up with, Kate Flannery's the name
Everyone knew her down on the main drag
Kate had a temper, but not like the other
The other she goes by the name Gallus Mag

Mag tucks her skirt up into suspenders
And holsters a flintlock onto her hip
On her wrist, a cudgel, strapped there with leather
And always cross words Mag wears on her lip
She delights in ejecting a riotous patron
She bites at their ears as she swings her baton
If the bludger's fool and he tries to fight back
With a quick tearing motion of her teeth he is gone

Once there was
A fight
On the floor
Was me
On my ear
Mag's teeth
Now my ear
In brine
In the pub
A bar
On the bar
A jar
In the jar
An ear
And that ear
Was mine

We're all in the mood for a drink, yes
You want a drink, don't you
Well go ahead down water street
To the Hole in the Wall, won't you
The company there is the city's best
If you like your company low
But if you go to the hole in the wall
The Hole in the Wall is a place I won't go

MOB OF TRAMPS

There's a fleet that comes up Hudson
Sometimes a hundred ship a day
And they carry dolly cargo
O up through the New York Bay
And they unload them on the wharf there
With an armored bull stand near
And when the shadows they grow longer
Then the river rats appear

Hi di di di diddle di di
Swing your arms and stamp your feet
Hi di di di diddle di di
If you're a chisler, punk, or cheat
Hi di di di diddle di di
Then there's a gang you oughta meet
Come and see them, come and see them
The mob of tramps from Charlton Street

There's a rowboat on North River
Lurking under the drydock
With its paddles wrapped in cotton
With its rowers hushed of talk
There's a sloop that's in the River
Filled with sailors and with swag
And the first will get a knifing
And the other gets the bag

There's are pistols on the sloop now
And a rifle in a hand
And they see the gang row near them
And the boatswain gives command
A volley sends up clouds of smoke
And stabs holes into the brine
And the gang they stop their rowing
And say to hell with you this time

A gang that busts a blagging
Is a gang that do not eat
And it's a hungry crew of wharf rats
Shivering on Charlton Street
What's the use of all that plunder
O out on the Hudson Boats
For a gang ain't got a leader
O they need Sadie the Goat

Hi di di di diddle di di
Swing your arms and stamp your feet
Hi di di di diddle di di
They are tired, sore, and beat
Hi di di di diddle di di
Then there's a gang you oughta meet
Sadie, Sadie, come and see them
The mob of tramps from Charlton Street

THE LONG BLACK SLOOP

Well its name was Old Nick's Sailor
And was then called Vicious Wretch
And I want it and I want it
How I want that two-mast ketch
There it sits out in the harbor
Just becalmed out in the soup
And I want it and I want it
How I want that long black sloop

Oh it has a figure on it
Carved and hanging from the bow
It's an angel colored gold but
I want to paint it black somehow
It has topsails and has mainsails
Hang down from masts in loops
And I want to paint them black too
How I want that long black sloop

I have a mob to take it over
We have boats and oars and spine
And I will own the Old Nick Sailor
The Vicious Wretch it will be mine
We will row out there in silence
O a rough and ready troop
And I will have it I will have it
I will have that long black sloop

THROW HIM OVERBOARD

There was Pike who was a sailor
And we bound him up in cord
And took him from his bed
And we carried him then toward
Our ship that was in the river
Just outside the auld fourth ward
We didn't know how to sail it
And so it stayed there that way moored
We then demanded that he teach us
But our demands old Pike ignored
But this is a city full of sailors
So we threw him overboard

Orvand was a sea dog
Norway his native land
He'd been a sailor since a boy
He was an rugged sailing hand
We caught him with a bobtail
Just exactly as we planned
And carried him then to the sloop
To make our one demand
But he spoke Norwegian
Which we couldn't understand
So we tied his hands with rope
Overboard then went Orvand

Mick he swabbed the decks
So we tossed him in the sea
Palmer was a galley cook
So he followed in Mickey
Hugo worked a dredge ship
A quick drop was his reward
And Tim, Liam, and Danny
All of them went overboard

If the Hudson it has risen
Now an inch or two inch high
It's filled up now with sailors
Who our sloop they dropp-ed by
One might know how to furl the sails
That would keep him briefly dry
If he didn't know the gunter line
The time would come to to say goodbye
It takes a lot to learn a sailor
It's an education, aye
But throw enough sailors overboard
You'll learn it, by and by

STONY POINT

There's a small town perched on
The banks of the great Hudson
Just north of old Haverstraw
There's a few farmers out there
Maybe too few to mention
And the darkest cave you ever saw
There's a lighthouse near town
On a forgotten battlefield
Where a mad general once beat Washington
There's a dark boat a drifting
Into the town of Stony Point
Prepared to take the town by knife and gun

Sleep well, Stony Point, sleep well
Sleep well, old town, sleep well

There's a day that's gone by
Since the ship docked that night
And a mob of rowdy bludgers swarmed ashore
There are two houses burnt
And three more still burning
There are five farmers missing maybe more
They got them on the black ship
And have demanded a big ransom
And swear they'll walk the plank unless it's paid
And every Stony Point man
Shakes his head and can't believe it
And collects what ain't been stolen in the raid

Pay up, Stony Point, pay up
Pay up, old town, pay up

There's a river named of Hudson
And a river named of Harlem
And there are hundreds of small towns along the shore
There's a black ship a-sailing
North and South upon the water
There are five farmers missing, maybe more

A ROVER'S CALENDAR:
JANUARY AND FEBRUARY

JANUARY'S rivers are icey
And we can't sail worth heck
Liam gets an idea
And makes a brothel on the deck
Forty sailors every hour
Served by 15 dollymops
Who picked every pocket
And stashed the booty in their tops

FEBRUARY brings a blizzard
And we docked us in a cave
And started up a pub there
Called the Shepherd's Lonely Grave
We warmed it with a barrel fire
And served whiskey to the dregs
And if they refused to pay their bills
We broke each of their legs

A SPENDING WE WILL GO

Hi ho
Let's go spending go
We've coin enough to spend, mates
Every man
To Manhattan
Let's shop until the end, mates

Crow Dan
Is a fancy man
He's a regular dandy now, mates
Hat, vest
Nosegay on his breast
He's the prince of the slough, mates

Nick the Boar
Has a taste for whores
He'll do a dozen every night, mate
Mornings he woke
Completely broke
Happy and quite tight, mate

Every thieving mutcher
At this here port of call
They got pockets full of stealing
And it's time to spend them all

Me I looks
For penny books
Telling of adventure and of crime, mate
At night I dreams
Of dodgy schemes
To pass away me time, mate

Hi ho
Let's go spending go
We've coin enough to spend, mates
Every man
To Manhattan
Let's shop until the end, mates

A ROVER'S CALENDAR: MARCH AND APRIL

MARCH it is a chilly month
And the ice cracks like a shot
We spend it robbing farmhouses
Of all of what they got
For a while we steal livestock
And stow them below deck
We forgot that cattle defecate
And it made the ship a wreck

APRIL it gets warmer
But the days are filled with rain
It's too messy to go raiding
But we gots Tim McCain
Tim was once a printer
And Tim can counterfeit
But his money looks like newsprint
And we dare not go spend it

FATHER BLUE

Father Blue
In an old canoe
Asked to come aboard
We told him nooo
He insisted
And tho we resisted
You can't say no to
Father Blue

Father Blue
Spoke to the crew
Bible in his hand
Opened to Luke 2
And on the waves
Our souls to save
We listened to
Father Blue

Some say soul's for saving
Some say soul's for Hell
Some say there ain't no soul at all
What Father Blue say I can't tell
He spoke to flinty sailors
Who sailed a sinful route
And they thanked Blue for his preaching
And they helped Father Blue get out

Father Blue
In his old canoe
Shouted of heaven
As we bid him adieu
We admired his persistence
But made haste to get distance
And were glad when lost view
Of Father Blue

A ROVER'S CALENDAR: MAY AND JUNE

MAY we go out hunting
All aboard they want to try
We shoot racoons up near Peeksill
And deer near Albany
The ship is filled with antlers
And fur on each crew man
And all it's smelling rotten
As none know how to tan

JUNE we find a mansion
In Cortland's rolling hills
The owner has 30 rooms
The owner owns the mills
We lock him in the cellar
And stay there for three weeks
We drink up all his wine and we
Sell off his antiques

ALONG THE OLD JACKLINE

I grew up in a city
Crowded houses crowded roads
I never saw the country
Where the New York Rivers flowed
I never knew no quiet
And it's quiet all round now
But for birds upon the wing
And the water on the prow

This land may stretch forever
Farther than ever I ken
And it's wild and it's bonny
And it ain't been touched by men
Behind me there are smokestacks
And teeming miles of slum
Ain't a daffy trace of it here
Tho with me now it come

Ain't a one aboard but me now
Along the old jackline
Alone here in the gloaming
In this balmy summertime
All the rest have gone ashore
To have a merry row
But a merrier time I can't recall
Than the one that I have now

A ROVER'S CALENDAR: JULY AND AUGUST

JULY it is humid
And the river fills with flies
Who board the ship in thousands
And buzz around our eyes
The bite us when we're working
And bite us when we sleep
And though we kill a million
They bite us till we weep

AUGUST we go swimming
In the Harlem's muddy depth
Some ain't never learned to swim
And swim themselves to death
We wrap them up in blankets
As would be their final wish
And then we drop them in the Harlem
Where they can feed the fish

THE SLAVES

By the shores
We saw a fire
A hundred men gather round
They sang a song
A Quaker prayer
A calm and stately sound
There was with them
A dozen who
Had faces black and feared
They stared at us
With widened eyes
As up the Hudson O we steered

We looked at them
They looked at us
And Billy Potts laughed and said
It's slaves it's slaves
Come way up north
They fled he said they fled
Some said we should
Go get them now
And collect an ample ransom
For a dozen slaves
The slavers pay
A reward both full and handsome

Nah said Pete
Who was a boy
But a bright and fighty lad
What are they them
But just like us
Going north and going bad
Some disagreed
But not enough
As we had our own affairs
And they slaves they watched
As we passed on
And sang their Quaker prayers

A ROVER'S CALENDAR: SEPTEMBER AND OCTOBER

SEPTEMBER is a cheery month
As we raid a brewery
And we drink a drink of ale now
And then drink two or three
Some lads get mean when they get drunk
And fight for no reason
We wrap their bodies in blankets and
Drop them in the Hudson

OCTOBER some go treasure hunt
Up near old Haverstraw
There's legends of a murder there
And a fortune hid from law
They say it's in the forest near
Lake Kanawauke
10 lads take pistol and shovel and
None return that day

SAILING DEAD

Topsy Boy is hard as they get
And he don't usually cry
But he's weeping like a bantling
And he will not say why
The other boys are talking
Julking Mike he talks the most
He says they all seen an awful thing
He say they seen a ghost

And it's heave away heave away
Heave away me ragged dogs
With a tale of the sailing dead
And a pint of Navy grog

Bunko Jim says look at the mast
And all looks up just then
And a cloth it blows from the mizzen sail
And it ain't there again
Gaffing Tom says late at night
There are whispers from below
And if you listen close they curse and say
To the briny lads you'll go

And it's heave away heave away
Heave away me ragged dogs
With a tale of the sailing dead
And a pint of Navy grog

Some say leave the ship, mates
Some say burn it down
Some say we're wrong to sail it
Some think all will drown
Some say we are not pirates
But townies away from town
But what I say is what matters
And I says batten down

There are tales of a massacre
That befell an early crew
And they say the dead are restless still
And the boys swear all is true
I say them ghosts are welcome here
Underneath the pirate's jack
In all me life I've seen plenty dead
And not a single one come back

A ROVER'S CALENDAR: NOVEMBER AND DECEMBER

NOVEMBER an illness takes the ship
We clutch our heads and cry
And empty our stomachs out of us
And 30 of us die
In fever we do awful things
Too awful to tell
We were a ship headed up a river
Now we're a ship headed to hell

DECEMBER the crew is down to 10
December will be our last
A year since we set out to sail
A year before the mast
We'll end it all with one last raid
And claim one last reward
And then we will sink the long black sloop
And return to the Fourth Ward

THE FARMERS

The farmers have got fighty
The farmers they got chapped
They ain't in no cheery mood
They're sick of being kidnapped
And farmers have got balers
And farmers have got gun
And when farmers now see pirates
They set them all to run

The Yonkers hands
Shot from the land
Them at Dobbs Ferry
Was quite contrary
At Irvington
They fired all the guns
And at Tarrytown
They nearly shot us down

The farmers have got vicious
And the farmer they got mean
They brought out men with cannon
The biggest any had seen
They aimed it at the river
And let the cannon roar
And shot holes in the long black sloop
And then shot holes some more

Up in Beacon
They howled Mohican
While in Hyde Park
They left their mark
Up in Troy
They armed man and boy
While Mt. Pleasant men
Shot at us again

The farmers they got murderous
They called for hangings and whip
So we decided to call it quits
And we burned and sank our ship

RATS 2

If you wanted sport
Some merry merry sport
There once was the Sportmans Hall
But Kit Burns is dead
And the pit's shut down
And the rats are scattered all
What was once a pub
For a sporting man
Now has a choir behind the bar
And a preacher preaches
Of the wages of sin
As to the sinner, there they are

Sing hey ho for dead Kit Burns
And hey for the Sportmans Hall
A good priest will save 100 souls
And the best will save them all

OBITUARY OF GANGS

Bowe Brother Jack who served all the gangs drinks
Killed his wife in a fight and died in the clink
Jimmy Corcoran he did aid and abet
He died in his home, shriveled with regret

Daybreaker Bill shot a man in the brig
They made him a noose and hung him up like a pig
Dutch mob's **John Irving** was generally quick
Until caught and then cut by Johnny the Mick

Little Kishky was with Crazy Butch for a time
But he fell out a window rehearsing a crime
Danny Lyons the Whyo was always a wreck
Killed a man for a whore and was hanged by the neck

Mike Abrams he went to war with the Tong
He died as most die who can't get along
Peter Mitchell became a religious chap
Hanged himself in his bar from a whiskey tap

Charles Livin he swore he never would hang
He was ambushed and killed by the Gopher Gang
Johnny Dobbs he stole millions all in one stroke
He squandered it all and Johnny died broke

James Ellison went and shot at Paul Kelly
Jim died in a madhouse, a lunatic felly
Dutch Heinrichs found prison was bad for his brain
He also went mad and he died insane

Old Shakespeare was kind and unusually chipper
Dead in the bowery, by, they say, Jack the Ripper
Jim Farrell the drunk, who they say was my father,
Went blind from the drink and then died without bother

The city is empty of all that I known
And it's a worser city now that I live it alone
There's none that remain that remember a boat
A gang and a pirate named Sadie the Goat

THE HOME FOR ERRING AND WAYWARD WOMEN

If you were a sporting man
And lived a sporting way
And wanted you a sporting house
Where the sporting gals are gay
You got you a book a blue blue book
And you read that bawdy sheet
And you went you went to the fourth ward
And you went to Water Street

This was the way when I was a girl
I've been gone and it ain't the same
All the sporting houses are shut down
Ain't no more of the sporting game

There's a house a wicked wicked house
On the corner of Dover
Now it is a house for wayward gals
And its wickedness is over
This was me home when I was a gal
This is where I learned me trade
The blue book it would once lead here
For sins both free and paid

This was the place when I was a girl
But it ain't the place no more
Now it's a home for errant girls
Errant girls on every floor

And who should I find
Who should I find here
But the bouncer Gallus Mag
Who I ain't seen in a year
And she looks at me
And says I know you dear
You're the one that I fought
The one I took the ear

There's a story a story that I read
Of a pirate that sailed the sea
And I knew that I could that I alone could
Make a pirate out of me
But the tales they end with the pirate disappeared
I ain't disappeared at all
And here I am at Water and Dover
What once was a sporting hall

There was a time when I was a girl
But that time has passed me by
When I'd read in a book of an astonishing thing
An astonishing thing I'd try

Gallus Mag says
You wait right here
And she turns away
And she disappears
And then she comes back
Clutch a pickle jar near
And says this is yours
I kept your ear

There was a place when I was a girl
Where I had things to do
Now it's a place for wayward girls
And I am wayward too

THE BALLAD OF SADIE THE GOAT REPRISE

There's a figure doubled over
in the alley by the square
some wonder if she's breathing,
but they leave her lying there
none goes to see about her
none calls to her, none dare
though she's old and arthritic
and her clothes she ragged wear

and the body lies untouched
in an alley on a furrow
and the mother pulls her son away
saying come now lad let's go now
who was she he asks weeping
oh she says, oh, oh, oh now
she was a pirate she was a pirate
and that's all you need to know now

Made in United States
North Haven, CT
03 December 2025

83638437R00035